Night Lights

by
Lucy Jane Bledsoe

Marjorie L. Kelley, Ed.D.
Educational Designer

Beth Whybrow Leeds
Illustrator

Quercus Corporation
2405 Castro Valley Boulevard
Castro Valley, California 94546

Printed in the United States of America.
ISBN 0-912925-31-0

Contents

Kate leaves in the dead of night.

1

In the Dead of Night

Kate leaves the house by the back way. It is the dead of night, around 12:30 a.m. Without making a sound, she walks down the driveway. She is shaking all over. Not because she is scared. But because she knows that tonight she will start living the way she wants to live. Kate is taking things into *her* hands.

Kate stops at the end of the driveway. She turns to look back at the house one more time. All the windows are dark. The blinds are down. Her parents, big brother and small brother are sleeping.

Before she goes on, Kate looks into her big bag. There she has her brush, a blanket, a flashlight, Mrs. Moe's letter, the page of paper from Willy, and $22 for the bus. When she gets to L.A., all she has to do is find Willy. He will see to things then.

At the bus station, Kate goes up to the window to get a seat for the bus. The bus for L.A. leaves at 1:00 a.m. The man selling seats says the bus is about to leave. Kate gets on the bus only seconds before it leaves. There are only 6 other people on the bus.

"Where are you headed?" the bus driver asks her.

"L.A."

"What for?" he asks.

"I am going to see a friend," Kate answers.

The bus driver looks at her for a long time. Then he looks at her bag. "What makes you go at this time of night?"

"Why do you ask me all these things?" Kate says getting somewhat mad.

"Because," the bus driver says. He thinks for a second before he goes on. "You look like you are running away. And I don't want you to get hurt. You know, L.A. is a big town. It's not at all like this small town where you live. L.A. has over 700 times the people this town has."

6

"I know," Kate says trying to look as old as she can. "I have been to L.A. My parents and I went there on a trip in the fall. I know all about L.A."

"I see," the bus driver says. He shakes his head for a long time not saying a thing. And then he says, "I ran away years back when I was 15. I was mad at my parents. They did not know what was up and what was down."

"I am 17," Kate says, thinking that 17 years old is not at all the same as 15 years old. She turns away from the bus driver. He sounds like a good guy. But she knows he wants to talk her out of running away. And no one can do that. Kate now knows what she wants. And no one can stop her from getting it.

The bus moves down the highway fast. Kate sees groups of lights go by. She knows they pass town after town. It takes about 7 hours to get to L.A.

Kate thinks back on her house, parents, big brother and small brother. She is happy to get away from them. There has been a bad scene every night now for 6 weeks—screaming and all that. Her parents are having bad times. And Kate thinks they try to take it out on her.

7

And then 3 weeks back Kate's boyfriend started going out with her best friend. After that Kate started falling back in her studies. Everything that has happened to her this year has been bad.

The worst of all is Kate's small brother. He is only 10 years old and he is so *stupid*. All he does is go around with tears running down his face. And he makes things up. He always says Kate did something to him. "Kate did this to me! Kate did that to me!" Only about one out of every 10 things he says is true.

Kate thinks her big brother Ed is OK. He wanted her to move into his car shop. The shop is a small house in the back yard of her parents' house. Ed has all his car things in it. But he said he would move out all of his things if she would move in. That way she would be out of the house.

Out there she can play her records loudly. And she does not have to see anyone. Her parents said it was a good idea.

But Kate said "No way!" Where would Ed put all his car things? And besides, the shop is cold and does not have one window. Some living space that would be! And anyway, Kate does not want to be in her parents' back yard. She wants to get out of her parents' house, yard and town!

So Kate split for L.A. They will not know where she went. Kate does not think they would try to find her if they did know. Kate thinks about these things for a long time before she falls off to sleep.

"Do you have any $$$ for eating?" The bus driver is talking to her. Kate starts in her seat. She has been sleeping. She looks out the window and sees it is light now. And they are in L.A. "Take this," the bus driver says putting a $5 in Kate's hand. "You will have to eat."

"No," she answers. "I don't want help."

"What about going back?"

"I am not going back."

"Look," the bus driver says putting the $5 bill back in Kate's hand. "I drive these miles every other day. Tonight I take off for your town at 1:00 a.m. Meet this bus at the station. You will know this bus by the red letters on the side. It is the only bus with red letters. Meet this bus and I will take you back. And you will not have to give $22 for the seat. Any time you want—look for me."

"That is good of you," Kate says. "But I don't want help." Kate hands the $5 bill back to the bus driver and jumps off the bus. She walks out of the station into the daylight. Kate puts her hand over her face so she can see. It is a warm day in L.A. Now all she has to do is find Willy.

2

Kate Hits the Big Town

Kate looks in her bag for the paper from Willy. She knows Willy from the trip she and her parents made to L.A. in the fall. Her parents wanted to see the sights one day. But Kate did not want to be seen with them. And besides, Kate wanted to see other things than what they wanted to see. She wanted to meet TV people. So Kate went walking all around town, from street to street. She was looking for TV people. Most of them live in L.A. Kate was trying her best to sight one.

Most of all, Kate wanted to see May Louis. May Louis is on TV every night at 7:00. She does "What's Happening." She talks with people from all over the world about everything. Kate thinks that everything May Louis says is true.

And she writes books that Kate likes. They are the *only* books that Kate likes. Sometimes Kate thinks May Louis is talking right to her.

Kate's parents did not like May Louis. They said she was "one of these save the world people" (as they put it). "All talk," her parents said.

"It's more than you do to help people in the world!" Kate called back to them. Sometimes Kate turned on May Louis' "What's Happening" just to make her parents mad.

Anyway, that day in the fall (when her parents went sight-seeing) Kate went looking for May Louis. She did not see her. But she did meet Willy. She was looking in a shop window. And Willy just walked up to her on the street. And they started talking.

He said he was a photographer. Kate did not think he looked like one. He did not have any photography things with him. But then who knows what he was doing that day? Maybe he was on a big job all that night and was taking the day off. Kate started to like him right away because he talked all about TV people in L.A.

Willy said he worked for TV people all the time. *If you want to get into TV, living in L.A. is the best,* he said. *Anyone can find a TV job in L.A.,* he said. And that is just what Kate wants—to work in the TV field. She has wanted that for as long as she can remember. Now the time has come.

So Willy said for her to come to L.A. He said he knows someone who is big in L.A. She is called Sue Page and is a good friend of his. Willy said that maybe Kate can live with Sue when she gets to L.A. And she will help Kate get a job in TV.

Kate said she would not turn him down. She would be back. So he handed her a page of paper. It says where she can find him when she comes back. And Kate is on her way now. She looks at the paper. His hand-writing is not good. It says, "Willy." And then below that, "Blue Root." That's all.

"I can find that," Kate thinks out loud. Willy said the Blue Root was a restaurant where he went all of the time. Kate can just picture all the TV people there . . . she can't wait. Her time has come!

As Kate puts the paper back in her bag, she sees Mrs. Moe's letter. She takes that out and reads it. Mrs. Moe, a teacher at school, wanted to help Kate get into TV. She wanted to find a work-study job for Kate. With work-study she would not make a thing. She would have to work for nothing. But she would get to know TV work. And that would help her get a job in a year or more.

But Kate was not going to work for nothing. Not for a year or more! And not if she can go to L.A. and get into TV right away. Willy is a photographer and knows what he's talking about. Kate puts Mrs. Moe's letter back in her bag.

She does not head for the Blue Root right away. It is only 9:00 a.m. She has all day to get there—and all of L.A. to take in. And besides, some guy is on her tracks. He has been walking after her from the time she was off the bus.

As Kate turns down another street, she looks back at the guy again. He is good-looking, that is one thing. But why is he walking after her? Looking back, Kate starts walking faster.

The guy does not stop going after her. Kate walks faster and faster. The guy makes every turn she makes. What is happening?!

3

Working Together

Kate thinks she better just stop and see what this guy wants. And so she stops and turns around.

"Hi!" the guy calls out when she turns around. "Can I talk with you for a second?"

Kate waits for him to run up to her. He looks like he is about 17 years old. *Why don't 17-year-old guys look like this in my town?* Kate thinks.

"I am Dan," he says holding out his hand. "And right off the bat I want to say I will not—again, I will *not*—turn you in."

"Turn me in . . . ? What are you talking about? OK, who are you?" Kate backs up scared.

Kate talks with Dan, the guy from Kids and Parents Working Together.

"I am just a kid like you. I go to a high school in L.A. And I have a work-study job with a group called Kids and Parents Working Together. We try to help kids who run away. At the same time, we try to help the parents."

"Why are you after me? I am not going back."

"I am not *after* you," Dan says. "Your parents called us in L.A. 3 hours back. They are calling all over trying to find you. They wanted us to find out if you went to L.A."

"But—!" Kate gets ready to leave.

"Wait!" Dan says. "We will not turn you in. That is up to you. But we do ask you to call your parents. They have said they will not try to make you go back. They only want to be in touch—and to know you are OK. But you don't have to call if you don't want to."

Kate looks at Dan for a long time. It is a good thing for him that he is so good-looking, she thinks. Because that is the only thing that makes her not leave.

"Want to go get something to eat?" he asks. Then he laughs. "The group gives me $20 just to get something to eat. I bet we can find some good things to put away with $20."

Kate laughs with Dan then. The word "eat" makes her gut turn upside-down. She is ready for something good to eat, and now!

"OK," she says.

"I know a good restaurant on this street," Dan says. "Let's go there. We can talk."

They go and order just about everything on the menu. Kate eats and eats and eats.

"It looks like you ran away 5 days back by the way you eat!" Dan says.

Kate turns red and says, "I always eat this way."

Dan talks to Kate all about his job at Kids and Parents Working Together. He says he wanted to be the one to look for Kate at the L.A. bus station because he wanted to meet her. He is moving with his parents to her town in 6 weeks. And so he wanted to ask her all about the town.

Kate talks about her town. Right now she does not like it at all. But she thinks of some good things to say. Most of all, she does not want to stop talking with Dan. She can see that he likes her. Kate has on her best shirt and knows she looks good today.

They eat all they can. And then Dan gets up. He says he has to get back to school. Kate feels something fall in her gut. *I bet Dan is one of the "good kids" at school,* she thinks. Then she thinks that Dan gets all A's. He looks like all the kids on the yearbook at her school. And he looks like he works on the school news . . . She thinks he does not like her after all. Going out to find her and talk to her is only his job.

Out in the street they talk some more about Kate's running away. Kate says she will not call her parents. But she says Dan can write them a letter saying she is OK—but not saying where she is. And she gives him her word that she will call Kids and Parents Working Together every day.

But Kate does not say everything to Dan. She says only that she is going to be with a friend. She says it is an old friend. That is not true . . . but Kate doesn't want to give Dan all the story on Willy. She doesn't want to say that she wants to get into TV. She thinks he would think she is being stupid.

Kate starts down the street with Dan looking after her.

"Kate!" he calls after a second. She turns. "Can I call you when we move to your town?"

"I will not be there. Remember?" Kate laughs. "But you can come see me in L.A."

"I will call, just the same," Dan says. "When I get to your town, I will call."

4

Looking for Willy

Kate finds a phone book and looks up the Blue Root. By now it is 11:00 and she thinks she will head that way. After all, she can see L.A. as she walks. Kate finds the Blue Root in the phone book and starts to walk.

Kate walks and walks and walks. From time to time she has to stop in at a gas station to see where she is. L.A. is a big town, all right. All the people move fast with their heads down. No one looks up or stops to talk in the street. Everything is new to Kate.

All the same, Kate feels good. She wants to meet all of Willy's friends. And one of his friends, Sue Page, is going to get her a job in TV. Maybe it will only be a small job. But she can work her way up from there. And Willy said she can live with Sue for a time. When she finds Willy, it will all work out.

Kate stops in another gas station. A man there does not know the Blue Root. But he looks it up in a phone book. He says she is on the right track.

"Why do you want to go there?" he asks as he puts gas in a woman's car.

"I have a friend there," Kate says.

"Hold on to that bag," the man says. And Kate takes off again.

Kate has been walking for 3½ hours now. Her legs start to hurt. And this street does not look as good as the ones she was on before. Kate thinks that this is not the best side of town. There is not a house in sight where she is now. Just old shops. And everything looks so run-down.

For the 1st time Kate thinks that maybe she will not find Willy. Did he make all this up? Maybe he did not think she would come to L.A. Maybe he was only playing a game with her. This does not look like the side of town where she would find TV people.

22

Kate does not know what she will do if she does not find Willy. The Blue Root *is* in the phone book. But no one she talks to knows about the Blue Root. Would not people know about it if TV people went there?

What if she finds the Blue Root but Willy is not there? She did not think of these things before she went. Why not? There was something about Willy that made her think he only said true things. He did not look like someone who would play a game with someone's head. Willy would not do that to her . . . or so Kate thinks.

Kate holds back her tears. She is not going to give up on Willy now. She will find the Blue Root. And if he is not there, then she will think about what to do next. If she has to, she will wait for Willy at the Blue Root. She moves on, trying not to think about her hurting legs.

Kate walks and walks. She has been walking for about 7 hours when she just about trips over someone's legs. An old woman is seated on the walk. Kate sees that the woman is blind and has no teeth. She holds a can out to Kate.

"Do you have a coin for me?" she asks.

23

"No," Kate says. "I do not have one coin on me. But I am looking for the Blue Root. Do you know where that is?"

"Look up," the old woman says. "Over your head."

Kate looks over her head. She only sees an old, old run-down shop. It looks like an old restaurant. But it doesn't look like anyone is selling things there now. Then Kate sees some blue letters. This is what she sees: BL E ROOT. Kate thinks about what letter goes in the space.

This is the Blue Root?! This is not what Kate was thinking she would find. She was thinking the words "Blue Root" would be in flashing lights. And what about the people with shining faces? This is not the L.A. TV scene Kate was looking for. Maybe there is another Blue Root.

5

The Blue Root

Kate hits her hand on the window of the Blue Root. The blinds are down. And no one answers. So she walks in.

It takes a second for Kate to see. It is so dark in the Blue Root after being in the light outside. Kate waits a second so she can see. Then she looks around fast.

What a scene! The Blue Root is like a big, long hall. There is only one blue light. And a big, old TV is turned up loudly. Up on the sides of the hall are pictures. They look like they have been ripped out of books. There are some dishes around. Kate sees a woman making things to eat in the back. But this does not look like a restaurant where they *sell* things to eat . . . what is it?

Then Kate sees a circle of people at the end of the hall. They are seated below the one blue light. They are on old car seats that have been ripped out of cars. One guy is sleeping. Others are talking. The picture on the TV is not clear, and no one looks at it. Kate does not see Willy anywhere.

One man sees Kate come in. He looks up and says, "Who is that?"

"Who is who?" another man says walking out from the back. He looks over at Kate and throws his head back.

"Kate!" he calls out. It is Willy. Kate walks over to the group. She is so happy to see him. He is in town, after all. And he *does* remember her! Now she feels bad for thinking that maybe he would not be there.

"Hi, Willy. I made it," she says trying to look like she comes into L.A. all the time.

"Ready for the big time, is that it?" Willy laughs. "Let me start your introduction to L.A. This is Kate," he says holding up her hand. "And this is Kicker, Tad, Jake, Bob, Jim-Jim, Sue. And that is Dot over there. Dot runs the Blue Root. You know, she is selling

Kate meets Kicker and Willy.

things . . .things to eat . . . and other things." The group laughs with Willy.

Kate likes Willy's friends. They do not look like her friends. But they all look like good people. That makes her happier right away. Now she thinks that she likes the Blue Root . . . It's like no space she has seen before. She thinks it has some class.

But where does Willy live? Kate thinks. *Where do all these people live?* Kate looks at Sue for a long time. She does not look like someone who works in TV. But who knows about the L.A. TV scene? Kate knows it's another world—not like a thing she knows from her small town. She is new and will just listen. She can wait to see what's up.

"Kate wants to get into TV," Willy says.

"You are in the right town," someone says.

"Man, I have a good idea. Let's go into L.A. tonight. We can let Kate see the lights of L.A. All the people from the TV scene are all over Hammer Street these days."

"Now you are talking," Willy says. "What about it, Kate? Ready to hit the town?"

Kate wanted to eat something before she did another thing. But now she does not remember wanting something to eat . . . not now that they are talking about the TV scene. There's nothing she wants more than to see L.A. at night.

Kate holds her bag and is ready to go. But no one moves right away. They all talk and look at TV some more. So Kate throws down her bag. She starts to talk with everyone.

"You are the Sue who works in TV?" Kate asks.

"Me? TV? Don't kid around!" Sue laughs loudly. "Not me!"

"Where is Sue Page?" Kate turns to Willy. "Your friend in TV."

"Sue Page?" Willy says. "Sue . . . uh . . . that is right!" Willy's face lights up. "You can meet Sue. But not right now. We have the town to do, right? Who is going with us?"

Kicker and Sue say they will go. Dot and the others do not stop looking at the TV. And so the 4 of them—Willy, Kate, Sue, and Kicker—leave the Blue Root. Kate does not remember that she has not eaten in over 8 hours. She is as happy as she can be.

6
Night Lights

"Have a car?" Willy asks Kate as they leave.

"A car? No . . . I . . . ."

"That is OK. We can try my car," Willy says.

"Are you saying that old can *moves*?" Kicker asks.

"Sometimes," Willy laughs.

They all walk down the street to Willy's car. It takes a long time for Willy to get it started. But he does and they take off.

Kate feels light-headed from not eating for so long. By now it is 9:00 at night. And she has not eaten all day long. But she doesn't want to say it. What stopped her from taking that $5 from the bus driver? *That was stupid,* she thinks as her gut calls out loudly.

But Kate stops thinking about this when they get to town. Willy stops the car. The group gets out and starts to walk.

So this is L.A. by night! Kate wants to see everything all at the same time. Her head is going around and around in a circle. All the shop windows are lighted up. Kate wants to stop by every one to look. She sees a skirt she wants. And other things. There are good-looking people everywhere. And they all have on about $1000 from head to shoe.

It will not be long before I have these things, Kate thinks. *I only need a job in TV. Then I can get everything in these windows.*

"Let's take Kate over to Chet's Restaurant," Willy says to Kicker. Then he turns to Kate. "That's where all the TV people go. You will see them there tonight."

Kate just about dances over to Chet's Restaurant with Willy, Kicker, and Sue. *Is this happening to me?* she thinks, happy.

The restaurant has big windows. Kate can see everything from outside. They all stop and look in. The 1st thing Kate sees are all the good dishes to eat. Every one looks so good! But then Willy helps Kate remember that there may be TV people in there. She looks around at all the faces. Her look falls on one good-looking man in a blue shirt.

"Willy!" she calls out. "Is it true? Is that . . . Louis Brush? It is!"

Kate thinks Louis Brush is the best-looking guy on TV. And there he is . . . before her, living, walking, and talking. He is better looking than on TV!

"Let's go in," Kate says with her hands to her head. But when she turns around she sees that Willy, Kicker, and Sue have walked on. She runs after them and catches up. She talks so fast she can't get the words out. She says she wants to go into Chet's—Louis Brush is there.

"Are you out of your head?" The way Willy says this makes Kate feel stupid. What is wrong with wanting to go into Chet's? "You have to flash a $100 bill before they will *think* about letting you in there."

Kate thinks that it is good Willy, Kicker, and Sue did not see her jump up and down outside the window about Louis Brush. What a stupid way to be about some guy on TV. Kate thinks that she will be more together from now on. She does not want to do the wrong thing in L.A.

The night goes on. They walk and walk. Kate thinks her legs will fall off. But she does not say a thing. Willy, Kicker, and Sue take her to see all the sights. Her hurting legs do not stop her from having the best time she has seen in years. Kate takes in all she can.

By the time they get back to Willy's car, Kate is ready to sleep for hours. She falls to sleep going back in the car. What a night!

It is 3:00 a.m. when they get back to the Blue Root. Willy stops the car a street or 2 away from the Blue Root. No one talks as they all get out of the car. Kate is sleepy. But she does not know where she is going to sleep. They walk over to the Blue Root.

The same group is not in the Blue Root now. But a new group of people is there. They talk and laugh on the car seats. No one looks like he or she is in the TV field. These people do not look like the people down on Hammer Street.

"Can you take me to Sue Page's?" she asks Willy.

"At this time of night?" Willy laughs. And Kate sees that she has said something stupid again. "Come on, Kate. What would you do if someone headed over to your house at 3:00 a.m.? We will find a space where you can sleep."

Willy goes to the back of the hall to find Dot. Kate goes over and gets seated with the other people. She will talk and just be one of them. She doesn't want to look like she doesn't know what to do.

After some time Willy calls Kate over. She goes back to where he is with Dot. "Want something to eat?" he says putting out a dish of something for Kate.

That was good of him, Kate thinks. She eats fast. Willy and Dot talk. Dot gets up and gets Kate something more to eat. Now Kate feels happy about being in L.A. Willy is looking after her. She is in good hands.

"Go meet some people," Willy says to her after she eats. "I will be out in a second."

Kate goes out to talk with the others on the car seats. It is not long before Willy comes out again.

"I have to go," he says as he comes up in back of her. He puts a hand on her head. "Look, I'll come back in the a.m. . . . at about 10:00, OK? Then I'll take you to see Sue. Does that sound all right?"

"But tonight . . . where?"

"You will be OK at the Blue Root. Dot is a good woman. She will not kick you out. See you!"

Willy takes off before Kate can get in another word. She does not want to sleep in this big, dark hall all night. Not with all of these people around . . .

7

Sleeping in the Blue Root

"Who are you with?" one man says getting seated next to her.

"With? I am not with anyone," Kate says. But in the next second she wants to take it back. She has to *think*—not just say everything that comes into her head. But she does not know what to do now. She can't take it back. And so she talks with the guy some more. *Maybe he is OK,* she thinks. Maybe he can help her out in some way.

The guy is warm—more warm than Kate wants him to be. As he talks, she sees his hand move over by her leg. He throws his other hand over the back of the car seat she is on. Kate is thinking about a way to move away from him. But then she sees Dot walking her way.

36

"OK, you guys," Dot says. "Out. Time to go. It's 4:00 a.m."

"What?" Kate looks up. "We have to leave?"

Some of the others laugh at Kate. "What did you think?" one guy asks. "Did you think we all *live* at the Blue Root?"

The man who was next to Kate takes her hand. He looks into her face with warmth. "Look," he says. "I know where you can sleep tonight. Come with me."

Kate looks around. Where can she go but with this guy? Dot is kicking them all out. She can't sleep in the street. But Kate does not like the looks of this guy . . . What is she going to do?

Just then Dot walks up and takes Kate's hand away from the guy.

"She can sleep at the Blue Root," Dot says giving the guy a long, grave look. "You others, out! Now."

The others all leave. And Dot walks around turning everything off. Kate does not know what to say to her. She is happy she is saved from that guy.

"I have a blanket," Kate says trying to be of help. "I'll get it." She looks around for her bag. "My bag . . . Where is my bag? I put it right on the seat there . . ."

Dot stops what she is doing. She puts one hand on her side. She looks at Kate and shakes her head.

"Girl," she says. "What makes you think you can leave your bag in a restaurant on this side of town for 6 hours . . . ? Leave and come back to see it again? Where have you been all these years?"

"But in the bag there is only my blanket and brush and—"

"There was only your blanket and brush. No more," Dot says. "You better go on back to that small town you are from. You are not going to make it in L.A. That is as clear as daylight.

"Look," Dot goes on talking to Kate. "Where do you think you are going to sleep after tonight? Not in *my* restaurant. They come looking for kids who run away all the time. And if they find you in my restaurant, they will give me the axe right away—that will be the end of the Blue Root. Then what? Where do I go after

38

Dot shakes her head at Kate.

that? I just can't house every kid who comes by and is running away."

Kate listens to Dot. Then she says, "But Willy is going to take me to a friend of his. After tonight I can sleep there. I know it will take some time to get a job. But his friend will help me. Then I will be all right."

"Willy," Dot says and shakes her head again. "That Willy." Then Dot turns to look at the TV before turning it off. A good-looking woman is reading the news. Kate looks and listens at the same time.

"And this is Sue Page, saying good night for CBS nighttime news," the woman says just as Dot turns off the TV.

"That's her!" Kate calls out to Dot. "Did you hear? That is Sue Page, Willy's friend!"

"Mmmmm. Is that so," Dot says walking to the back of the Blue Root. She lives in a small space in back of the long hall. She gives Kate a blanket and says she can sleep on the car seats.

Kate is scared to be the only one out there. But now that she has seen Sue Page, she feels better. Sue Page reads the nighttime news. That's a good start—she can get Kate a job if she wants. And being a friend of Willy's will help.

Now the TV is off. And there is not a sound. Kate puts the blanket over her head. She thinks about Willy. The way Dot said the word "Willy" made Kate scared. What's wrong with Willy? He is not a bad guy. *He did leave me at the Blue Root tonight . . .* she thinks. *But that is only because he knows Dot will look after me.*

Kate starts to go to sleep as she thinks about Willy. After all, Willy has been so good to her. And he has better things to do than take *her* around. She will have to wait to do things on his time.

But there are some things she doesn't get. Where does Willy live? And where are all his photography things? When does he work? Maybe he will not come to get her at 10:00 a.m. Kate feels so lost. What will she do if Willy doesn't come get her. She is scared.

Kate falls off to sleep thinking about Willy. Everything is so new in L.A. and at the Blue Root.

8

L.A. by Day

The next thing Kate knows, someone is shaking her leg. Her head feels like it is 100 pounds. She kicks her foot to get the hand off of it. She thinks it is her small brother.

"Get up," someone says.

"Go away," Kate says. "I want to sleep. Go away."

"What are you talking about, Kate! Get up. Let's go find you a job! And Louis Brush! And $1,000,000! Come on! What are you waiting for?"

Kate looks up. She starts to remember she is in L.A. and not in her town. And it's not her brother shaking her leg. It is Willy.

She jumps up laughing. Kate would like more sleep, but the 6 hours did her good. And she is happy that it was not her small brother shaking her leg.

Kate is ready to take on the world of L.A. today. She throws off the blanket. She looks around for her bag so she can get her brush. Then it hits her that she does not have the brush or bag by now.

"I can't go see Sue Page looking like *this*!" she says to Willy.

"Kate, you look better than you did. Let's go. She is waiting for us."

"She is?" Kate's face lights up. "Then you called her? She knows I am in town?" Kate is ready to go.

"No, I did not call her. But we are old friends. It is OK."

Kate gives Dot her blanket back. And she takes off with Willy. They get in his car. In the back seat Kate sees an old blanket. And she sees some pictures.

"Are these your photographs?" she asks Willy as they drive off.

"Photographs?" Willy looks back to see what Kate is talking about. "That is them," he says to her. "They are from *World News*."

"You have photographs in *World News*?" Kate asks. "Boy, that is big time."

"Some say so," Willy says hitting the brake to make a turn.

They drive for about ½ hour. Kate asks where he lives. And she asks when he works. But he does not answer. Then Kate feels bad for asking. What right does she have to ask him all these things?

So then she says to Willy that she has seen Sue Page on TV. But Willy does not answer. Kate does not know if he is listening at all. Willy stops the car. They are a long way from the Blue Root.

"We are by the street where Sue lives. Let's leave the car," he says jumping out.

"Does she live in a house?" Kate asks.

"I don't remember," Willy says. "But it's one of these on this street. We will just have to look for a time. I will know it when I see it."

"But she's your friend."

44

"That is right. But it's been a long time. See the windows up there? One of them is Sue's I think. Let's go in."

"In *this* old house?" Kate is trying to be brave. And she wants to think it is true that Sue Page lives there. But no one in the TV field would live in a house like that! They go up to the house.

"Let me do the talking," Willy says. He pounds on the house. And they wait. No one answers. Willy pounds again. After a long time an old woman looks out a side window at them.

"What do you want?" she says.

"I am a photographer from *World News*," Willy starts to say. "And—"

"You can't take no pictures!" the woman screams in their faces. "What do you think this is, anyway? People *live* in my house and there is nothing to take pictures of—"

"Wait! Wait!" Willy calls out to stop her screaming. "I don't want to take any pictures. I am looking for Sue Page. Does she live in this house?"

"Sue Page? I don't know no Sue Page." The woman goes in the house and that is that.

9

Willy Gets Mad

Willy laughs. He throws his hands up over his head. "You know these TV people. They move all the time. Always on the go!"

"But Willy!" Kate says. She is getting scared. They have to find Sue. She is the only one who can help Kate get a job. "You said you know her! You said you know where she lives! You said she is your friend!" There are tears on Kate's face. She is starting to see Willy for what he is.

"You said! You said! You said! What is this?" Willy turns on Kate. He is mad in a flash. "What do you want me to do? Look. I can't always look after you. I have better things to do. I am trying to help. But if you are going to be like this . . ."

"I . . . I am not trying to make you mad," Kate says. She brushes her tears away. Without Willy, she does not have anywhere to go. She cannot let him leave her. She can't let him get mad at her. "I only wanted . . . I wanted to find Sue before night. I don't have anywhere to go tonight."

"OK, OK," Willy says, his face looking not so red. "We will find her. But give me time. This is only the 1st house. It's around this street. We only have to look."

Kate and Willy go to the next house. It is a shop. But people live over the shop. They go up to ask about Sue Page. But no one answers at the shop. And so they go on to the next. And the next. And the next after that. No one knows anyone called Sue Page. Kate and Willy go from house to house. And from shop to shop. They walk and look for 3 hours.

Kate is scared. She doesn't want to make Willy mad. But she can see that Sue Page is not a good friend of his. That is clear! He does not know where she lives. But they have to find her just the same. If they look, they will find her in time. L.A. can't be that big.

But at 1:00 Willy stops and puts a hand to his head. "I have to go do something, Kate," he says. "Why don't you go look around. Have a good time for an hour or 2."

"But—"

"Go about one mile down that way. And then over one street. There are some good shops and windows there. You will like looking around. And then, when I have more time, we can look for Sue Page some more."

"But Willy!" Kate says. "I have to find her by dark—"

"Don't start that again," Willy says. "I don't have time for that. Meet me at the Blue Root at 8:00. We will find her by dark. Maybe I can look some without you. That will work better. And save time. Then tonight I will take you there. OK?"

Kate only gives him a long, dark look. She holds in the way she feels. She cannot say that she is mad. Or that she is scared. That will only make him more mad. And then maybe he will not meet her tonight. Kate sees Willy looking at her for a long time.

48

In the next second Willy's face lights up. He takes her hands and dances around her in a circle. "Think of it, Kate!" he calls out. "Flashing lights! TV! $1,000,000! We will find it all for you!" He does not stop dancing in the street with Kate. She doesn't know what to do but to just let him take her around and around in a circle.

This time Willy's words do not take in Kate. She wants to try to laugh. But she only gets out a small sound. Now Willy stops laughing and dancing. He takes Kate's face in his hands.

"I can see you do not think what I am saying is true," he says. "You have to think better of me than that. You are in good hands. Now go off and have a good time. And meet me at 8:00."

Kate starts to walk. She goes one mile down, like Willy said. And she goes over one street. She sees where she is now. Hammer Street is only the next street up. Kate thinks she will walk to Hammer Street.

By now she would like something to eat more than any other thing. And she would like to get some sleep. Kate is feeling down. What is she going to do? What is she going to eat before she gets a job. She did not think of these things before.

Kate heads for Hammer Street. There she wants to look at the good-looking shop windows. But she walks with her head down. As she goes, she brushes something. A nail catches her shirt. It rips her shirt. There is a long tear. And it was her best shirt. Kate goes over to a shop window to look at new shirts.

But the 1st thing Kate sees is not shirts. In the window she sees a face looking back at her. "Is that me?" she asks out loud. What a sight! Kate has been without a brush for 2 days now. And she looks like it! And there is a big dark circle on each side of her face. And there is no light in her look. Her face was clear 2 days back. Now there are red dots all over her face. Kate looks like she has lost 5 pounds. And the big rip in her shirt looks bad.

Kate can just hear what her mother would say, "Your looks would raise the dead!" And this time it is true, Kate thinks. The worst is the way her teeth feel. She has nothing to brush them with. Kate thinks about what she would look like without any teeth—like the blind woman who lives in the street by the Blue Root.

50

She turns away from the window and walks over to the other side of the street. There is a big yard or field. And in it is a small lake. People are out walking their dogs. One man is walking his baby. Kate sees another man looking in a big can for something to eat. Looking at him makes her hands shake. She better get a job fast. Or she will be next . . .

10

May Louis

On the other side of the small lake Kate sees a big group of people. They look like high school kids. Kate starts walking that way. She would like to talk with someone who is in high school—it has been a long time.

Then Kate sees that the group of kids is around someone. Who are they all trying to talk to? Kate looks and looks as she walks. Then she stops fast. Is it . . . It is! It is May Louis from "What's Happening!" If there is anyone Kate would like to meet, it is May Louis. Kate starts to run over there.

She gets up to the outside of the group. They are all holding paper out to May Louis. And she is writing something on each paper. Kate sees that it is a high school class. They will leave after they get May Louis to write on their pages.

Kate waits off to the side of the group. And one by one the kids leave. Some look at Kate as they go. They look her up and down. Kate feels their looks. Other people have looked her up and down before. But this time it is not the same. Kate can remember what she looked like in the shop window. Do they think she lives in the streets? Like the woman with no teeth . . . ? Or like the man looking in the can for something to eat . . . ?

The kids all leave and Kate sees May Louis start to walk on. Kate starts to call out for her to wait. But she holds back. She does not want May Louis to see her looking like this. She walks in back of May Louis for a long time trying to think what to do.

"Is there something you want?" May Louis turns and asks after a time.

Kate gets red in the face. She walks up to May Louis. "I only wanted to say hi. I have read all of your books. And I look at 'What's Happening' every night on TV. Or I did, that is."

May Louis asks Kate if she has run away.

"That is good to hear," May Louis says looking Kate up and down like the high school kids did. "Why don't you look at 'What's Happening' now?"

"I . . . you see. I don't live with a TV now." Kate feels something pounding in her gut. Her face feels warm. It feels like May Louis' look goes right in her and out the back side.

"Have you run away?" May Louis asks.

What makes her ask that? Kate thinks. She hit it right on the mark. She always does—on TV, in her books, and right now. Kate thinks May Louis can read what's going on in people's heads.

"I guess so," Kate says. She does not know what May Louis will do. But May Louis does not turn away. She looks at Kate for a long time, lost in thinking. Then she starts to ask Kate things. She wants to know why Kate ran away. And she wants to know what she feels about it now. And what she is going to do. And what she is going to eat. May Louis goes on and on with the things she wants to ask. Kate doesn't know why she wants to know all about her. But she answers as best she can. She will do

55

everything May Louis says—or just about everything.

"Let me say something to you," May Louis says. "It's not up to me to say a thing about the way you live. But I want to do a 'What's Happening' on kids who run away. And I would like you to be on it."

"Is this true what you are saying?" Kate wants to jump up and down she is so happy. May Louis wants her to be on 'What's Happening'! Just think . . . talking with May Louis on TV.

"There's one catch," May Louis says holding up a hand. "It will only work if you go back to your parents' house. I am not trying to make you go back. That is up to you. But I cannot take you on TV if you are not 18. I have to have something in writing from your parents."

"No way," Kate says then, shaking her head. That is the one thing she will not do for May Louis. "I am not going back. And I will not ask them—my parents—for a thing."

"It's up to you," May Louis says again. "But if you go back, give me a call. I want to put it together in the next 3 weeks. You *have* run away. So you would know what you are talking about. And I like the way you talk. You are good with words. I think you would be good on 'What's Happening'."

May Louis gives Kate some paper. "This is where you can call me," she says. "And take this." She puts a $20 bill in Kate's hand. "That will get you on the bus."

"No, it will not," Kate says. "It's good of you to think of me. But I am not going back to my parents' house."

"Then take the $20 and get something to eat, OK?" May Louis puts her hand on Kate's face with a light touch. "And maybe I'll see you another time."

Kate does not move as May Louis leaves. She doesn't know what to say or do. She feels bad. She wants to be on 'What's Happening' with May Louis more than any other thing she can think of to do. But she just cannot go back to her house. Kate feels so bad.

She takes off her shoe. She puts May Louis' paper and the $20 bill in her shoe. Then she puts it back on. Kate starts to walk back to the Blue Root. It's a long way. And she has to meet Willy at 8:00.

11

Heading Back to the Blue Root

Kate heads into the 1st restaurant she sees. This is not the cheap side of town. But she has to eat before she does another thing.

After eating, Kate has $13.47. She puts it in her shoe and starts walking. She walks and walks. L.A. is so big. She knows it is a long way to the Blue Root. She and Willy went ½ hour in the car to get to this street. Walking, that will take hours. And it is 7:00 by now. Kate's legs hurt again.

She has to do something. There is a phone on the street. Kate goes to it. She calls for a car. She has $13.37 after the call. It will not take all of that to get back to the Blue Root. It only takes ½ hour for a car to get there.

Kate gets seated on the walk and waits for the car to come. The car gets to Kate fast. She jumps in. Kate says for the driver to take her to the Blue Root. And she gives him the street.

The driver hits the gas. And the car jumps out. Kate sees that it reads $3.00 just to get in the car. They drive and drive. Time goes by fast. Kate sees that ½ hour is over. Where are they going? She has not seen this street before. Now it reads $7.84.

Kate puts a hand ready to get out. She is scared by the way this guy is driving the car. He goes 60 miles an hour right in town. The car screams around turns. Kate can see that this guy is not taking her back to the Blue Root. She thinks they are going around in a big circle.

"You better let me out," Kate says after a time. She is scared.

"Why?" he ways. "We are not at the Blue Root."

"I only have $13," she says. "It says $10 now."

The man hits the brake fast. He turns the car to the side of the street and stops. By now Kate is shaking. The man throws his hands up over his head and starts to call out at her loudly.

"Look, kid. The Blue Root is a long, long way from here. You only have $13? Why did not you say so at the start? I am driving all over town for you and you only have $13! Trying to rip me off, are you?"

"But," Kate says. "It only takes ½ hour to get to the Blue Root from where we started. I just did it in another car. That is all it takes!"

"Look, kid. I drive this town 24 hours a day. Don't think you can teach me about driving. You want to get to the Blue Root or not?"

Kate does not answer.

"Answer me, kid!"

"I have to get to the Blue Root," Kate is trying to say out loud. But she can only make a small sound.

"OK, then. Give me the $13 now. And I'll take you there. But I want you to know I have lost about $10 by doing this."

Kate's head falls back on the seat. She knows he is getting the best of her. He turns off the thing that gives a reading on what she has to give him. Kate takes the $13 out of her shoe. She hands it to him. She cannot make it in this town without help. She will get ripped off every day. But who is going to help her?

Kate does not look to see if this guy takes her back to the Blue Root. She only puts a hand over her face and waits. If things do not go right, Kate does not want to see what happens. After some seconds, she feels the car stop.

"This is it, kid. Get lost," the man says. There is no one in the world as cold as this guy, Kate thinks. But she is happy she is back at the Blue Root. It is something she knows, anyway. Kate jumps out of the car.

She runs in the Blue Root and looks around. As always, there is a group on the car seats. Most of them are looking at the TV. Kate does not see Willy with them. What if he doesn't come? It's just about 8:00. There is time before dark—about 1½ hours. But she does not want to be in the Blue Root with these others . . .

Kate wants to talk with someone. She goes to the back of the hall to look for Dot. Dot was good to her. Maybe she would talk with her for a time. She does not go into the space where

Dot lives. But she calls out, "Dot! Dot?" There is no answer. Dot is not anywhere to be seen.

Kate walks around the Blue Root looking at things. The seconds go by one by one. Kate knows that outside the light is about to go. She starts to think Willy will not make it. He was mad . . . maybe she did him in. By now it is 8:30. Kate thinks about walking around in the street after dark . . . only her. And that is what it is going to be . . . if she doesn't get help fast. Dot said she cannot sleep in the Blue Root another night.

Just then someone comes running in. Kate sees that it is Willy.

"I was on the wrong track, Baby," he says to Kate. "But I think I have her now—Sue Page, that is. You see, I was looking on the wrong street. I did not remember where she lived when she was my friend. But I remembered she lived on Burn Street. Now I find that there is *another* Burn Street. We will go over there in a second. Now, doesn't that make you happy?"

That *does* make Kate happy. But she doesn't like the way Willy is talking to her. Before he did not talk down to her like he does now. It's as if he wants to get her out of the way.

But she wants to laugh it off. She wants to look happy. So she starts talking to him about seeing May Louis.

"Who is May Louis?" he says without stopping to listen to any more of what she has to say. He jumps on a car seat and looks at the TV. In one second, he looks like he's in another world.

12

Kate Is Saved

Kate looks at Willy who is looking at TV. Why does he start looking at TV now? He said he knows where Sue Page lives. Why doesn't he take her there now? Kate does not want to ask and make him mad. She will have to wait.

Just then there is a loud pounding outside the Blue Root. Someone wants to be let in. Who can it be? Why don't they just come in?

"Come in!" someone calls out. But no one comes in.

Dot comes out from the back to see who it is. *So she was there when I was calling her,* Kate thinks. *She did not want to talk to me.*

"Better not be the cops," Dot says shaking her head. "I don't want a scene." She looks over the group on the car seats. "Hear me?" No one answers her.

Dot walks over to see who it is. Kate is in the back of the hall where it is all dark. No one can see her. And she can only see a big, dark overcoat come in. Kate sees Dot talking with the man in the overcoat for a time.

"Willy!" Dot calls out. "I think this guy is looking for you."

No one moves but Willy. He gets up to go talk to the man. Kate waits back in the dark of the hall. She does not move. The man does not talk loudly. But she can hear Willy talk.

"No," Willy is saying. "I have not seen her. No, no one around who looks like that."

The man asks other things and Willy says "no" over and over. But the man does not leave. After a time Willy gets mad.

"Look, I said *no!*" Willy calls in the man's face. "Don't make me say it again."

Kate starts to think that the man in the big overcoat is looking for her. She walks that way to see him better. But she does not leave the dark side of the hall. She is thinking fast.

It is about 9:00 by now. She does not have anywhere to sleep. She doesn't have anywhere to go at all—day or night. Kate starts to think she is ready to give in. She wants to sleep and eat. She is just about to let the man take her away. Kate starts to walk over there.

By now Willy is just about screaming. "Who gives you the right to just walk into this restaurant? I said get out! There is no girl that looks like that. Hear me? Get out! Now."

Kate stops in her tracks. The big man takes Willy by the shirt. Is he going to hit him? The man throws Willy to one side. Then the man looks over at the car seats. The one blue light makes each face there shine blue. The man looks from one face to the next. Willy waits in back of him.

Kate wants to run over there and give in. But what if the man is a cop? Will they throw her out of school? Will they stop her from getting another job? And besides, now she has seen Sue Page on TV. She looked like a good woman, someone who would help her. Now they know where Sue lives. They are about to go see her. Now is not the time to turn back, Kate thinks.

Then Kate sees Willy in back of the man. He is shaking his head. Without making a sound, he says to Kate, *No! Don't do it!* Kate does not leave the dark.

The man turns and starts to leave. He has not seen Kate. He puts a hand out to Willy. Willy takes it and they shake. Willy hits him on the back like they are old friends. And the man starts to leave.

Just as he leaves, Kate sees another guy put his head in the Blue Root. He is looking for the big man in the dark overcoat.

"I'm coming, Dan," the man says and leaves.

"Wait!" Kate calls out to the man as he goes out. That guy who put his head in the Blue Root for a second was Dan! Kate will remember that face always. The man in the overcoat was there with Dan. They are from Kids and Parents Working Together. Now Kate sees what is happening.

"Wait!" Kate calls again. But the man is out of the Blue Root by now. Kate runs to go out after him. But Willy runs up to her. He gets a hold of her and stops her.

"Let go of me," Kate starts to say. But Willy isn't listening. He is laughing loudly.

"We did it!" Willy laughs. "I saved you, kid. That guy's job is to look for kids who run away. But we have put one over on him. You will be OK now. He will not come back."

"Willy," Dot shakes her head at him. "No more. I will not let you do that again. If they catch me with some kid who has run away . . . you know! That will be the end of the Blue Root. I will not have it!"

"It's all OK, Dot," Willy says. "It's all over."

"But, Willy!" Kate calls out as the tears start to fall down her face. "Where am I going to go tonight? Let go of me!"

"What a baby!" Willy says to her. "I was only trying to save you from the hands of the cops."

"They are not cops!" Kate says.

"You want to go back? Look, I did not know that. I was thinking you would make the big time in L.A. . . . not all this baby tears and all. Go ahead. Go find your friends. I am not stopping you. I did not ask you to run away. I was only helping you. Now look what I get for it!"

"Willy, I am not mad at you. And I am not giving up," Kate says. "But I don't have anywhere to go."

"Look, Kate. I give you an introduction to my friends. I give you an introduction to L.A. What more do you want?"

"I only want to know where I can sleep," she says.

"If you think you can sleep in the Blue Root, you are wrong," Dot says.

"Look," Willy says. "This is where Sue Page lives. I looked it up in the phone book. She is in a house at 173 Burn Street, on the other side of town. Go on. Find her."

Willy turns his back to her and heads over to the car seats. Dot turns to leave at the same time. But then she turns back to face Kate.

"Find this Sue Page if you can," she says. "I don't know her. And I don't know if she can help you. But look out, Kate. It would be best for you if you went back to your town—right now before something bad happens to you. I don't think you want to live like these people at the Blue Root."

Then Dot turns and walks away for good. Kate sees that no one at the Blue Root will help her. It is up to her now. She has to go find Sue Page. It is the only thing she can do.

Kate runs out of the Blue Root. She looks around for Dan and the man. They are not in sight. The dark is coming on fast. Kate knows she can't go back in the Blue Root. She looks up the street and starts walking.

13

Sue Page

Kate heads down the street. It is turning dark fast. She is scared. And every small thing makes her jump. She has no one now—no one but Sue Page. And Sue Page does not know her!

Kate feels bad for making Willy mad. After all, he is a photographer for *World News*. What time does he have for her? He has helped her all he can. He made her things to eat. And he talked Dot into letting her sleep one night at the Blue Root. He has a right to be mad at her. It was her idea to run away. Now she has to take things in her hands.

Kate heads for the bus stop. She thinks of Sue Page's face on TV. That makes her feel better. Sue Page looked like someone who knows what she's doing. She can help Kate. Kate gets to the bus stop and waits.

It is not long before a bus drives up. It stops and the driver waits for Kate to get in.

"What bus will take me to Burn Street?" she asks the bus driver.

"Where on Burn Street?"

"173 Burn Street."

"You can take this one. Get on," the man says. But Kate does not get on right away. "What are you waiting for? I don't have all night."

"I don't have the 75¢," Kate says trying to hold her head up. The bus driver looks her up and down. Then he hits the gas and takes off.

Kate holds back her tears. She wants to let them go. But tears will not help her get to Burn Street. Kate is scared. She has no one and doesn't know what to do.

Kate waits for the next bus. There has to be another one within the hour. And one does come in about one hour.

The bus stops for her like the other one did. Kate looks at the woman in the driver's seat for a long time. She is scared to talk. Then she starts.

"I don't have the 75¢, but I have to get to Burn Street—tonight." Kate says all this looking at the woman's feet.

"Are you asking me to let you go without the 75¢?" the woman asks. "This is L.A., kid—"

"I know it's L.A.," Kate says. "That is why I can't wait out in the street all night like this. I'm scared. I have to get to Burn Street."

"OK. Get on. I'll take you."

Kate jumps on and falls back in a seat. She is so happy to be off the street. Now she is on her way to Sue Page's house. Will Sue be there at 11:00? Or does she work all night? Maybe she records the news before the time it goes on TV. Kate will just have to see.

"This is Burn Street," the driver calls out. "Are you getting off? Or did you just get on the bus to sleep?"

"I'm going. I'm going," Kate says jumping off. After she gets off the bus she turns around. She wants to say something to the bus driver. But the bus is going down the street. Kate throws up a hand to the woman and then starts walking.

All around Kate sees house after house. They are all good-looking with big yards. There are big trees all over. "Now this street is more like it," Kate says out loud. "I can see TV people living on this street. Let's see . . . this is 280 Burn Street. It has to be one street down."

Face to face with the house at 173 Burn Street, Kate laughs she is so happy. She has made it—after 2 days of looking! Now, if only Sue Page is there at this hour, it will all be OK.

Kate walks up to the house. The lights are on. Everyone in the house is up. Kate can hear kids screaming and playing in the house. She goes up and hits the window. One of the kids looks up. The small girl starts to let Kate in. But then she stops.

"Look, Bob," the small girl calls to her bigger brother. "Look at this girl outside. She looks like a street woman."

"What are you talking about?" A woman runs into the hall to see what her kids are doing. Then she sees Kate out the window, waiting to be let in. The woman puts her kids in back of her and calls out, "Who are you?"

Kate feels her gut fall to her feet. The woman in the house is scared! In that second Kate can remember what she looks like now. Her shirt is ripped. She has not washed in days. She has no brush for her head or teeth. And she is face to face with Sue Page.

"I . . . I . . . I am a friend of Willy's."

"Willy who?"

"Willy, your friend, the photographer from *World News.*"

Sue Page's face looks like she has no idea who Kate is talking about. A man walks into the hall to see what's going on.

"I have some of Willy's photographs," Kate says getting out 2 photographs. The photographs are the ones from the back of Willy's car. Willy let her have them.

"What is it?" The man is now at Sue Page's side. He lets Kate in. And she gives him the 2 photographs. The woman talks to the man.

"She says someone called 'Willy' knows me. And these—she says—are his photographs in *World News.*"

"Can't be," the man says looking them over. "It says who did these photographs right below them. See there?"

Kate shakes her head. She sees that it does not say Willy. She feels stupid for not looking before. Maybe she did not want to know these photographs are not Willy's. Why did Willy say he did these photographs?

"But I think I may know your friend Willy," the man goes on.

"You do?" Kate says. Her face lights up.

"Remember, Sue?" The man turns to Sue. "A guy called Willy worked in the yard a year back. He said he was a photographer, but I did not think it was true. He liked to talk. We let him go after he ripped off a thing or 2. He lives in the street most of the time. And he sleeps in his car."

"That is right," Sue says. "I remember now." She turns to Kate. "This guy is leading you on. He is no photographer. I can't help you. You will have to leave right away. And don't come back to this house."

"But I am looking for a job in TV, and—" Kate starts out. But Sue, the man, and kids turn

76

and leave Kate outside. Willy was not their friend at all. These are not his photographs. And he does not live anywhere. Kate feels so stupid . . . and so lost.

That was it. Sue Page was her only hold out. Now she has nothing. She can't go anywhere but the street. Kate falls down in the yard next to Sue Page's house. She puts her face in her hands, letting the tears go.

14

Kate on the Run

An idea hits Kate. She jumps up like it's the 1st good one that has come into her head in days. She brushes the leaves off her legs. And then she starts running fast. She runs and runs. Now she knows what she's going to do. She is heading for town.

Kate passes house after house. From where she is she can look down on the town lights. At every turn, she takes the street that goes down—to the lights and town.

Kate feels the cold night on her face. There is a small wind. And a light rain starts to fall. But nothing stops Kate. She puts her face into the wind and rain. As she goes, she sees in the window of a house. It is 11:30 now. She has 1½ hours. Kate runs faster.

She feels like she can run for hours now. She makes it to town. It is not so cold there. She runs down one street and then another. Kate sees some people sleeping in the street. They would scare her other times. But she is not scared now. No one better try to touch her tonight! Kate would meet them face to face. She knows where she is going. And no one will stop her.

Next Kate passes over Hammer Street. She turns down the next street and then the next. Kate runs by the restaurant where she and Dan stopped to eat. She would like something to eat now. But her legs take her on to the next street and into the bus station. It is 1:00 a.m.

Kate runs into the bus station. She passes right by the window with the man selling seats. She heads for the other side of the station where bus after bus waits.

"Hold up there!" he calls after her. "You can't go out there in the bus driveway without a seat!"

"Make a bet?" Kate calls back. She runs into a group of people. They fall away to one side or the other. Kate jumps the rope and runs by the man holding the people back.

"Get back!" the man calls. "Someone stop that girl!"

Outside on the big driveway there is bus after bus waiting to take off. One big, long bus has just started up. It has red letters on the side of it. It heads out of the station, going faster every second.

Kate takes off after it. Out of the driveway, the bus starts down a big street. She runs after it. Kate sees the bus has a red light before it. She can catch it then.

But the red light turns in time. The bus goes on down the street. Kate runs so fast she feels like her head is going to split.

"Wait! Stop!" she calls after the bus. But town sounds are so loud no one can hear her. She can't run anymore. Kate falls onto the walk holding her sides. She looks after the bus. What can she do now?

Then Kate sees that the bus is not going so fast. It is getting off the street and stopping. Kate gets up again and runs another 150 yards to the bus.

She gets to it and looks up at the driver. It's him all right. It's the same driver who goes from

Kate jumps on the bus.

her town to L.A. and back. The bus driver doesn't say a word as she gets on the bus. He doesn't give her one look—and he doesn't ask for $22 for the seat.

Kate walks to the back of the bus. All the people look at her as she goes. She can hear one man talking to the woman next to him.

"Hear of an L.A. bus stopping for someone? Right in the street? What is this town coming to?"

"Something new every day," the woman says shaking her head. "The bus driver has to be new to L.A."

Kate falls into a seat and her head falls back. She made it. For a time, all she can think about is eating, sleeping, and washing. Then she starts to think about what it will be like going back.

Maybe Ed will let her have his shop like he said before. She can put in a window. And out there she will not have to listen to her parents screaming. And she can get away from her small brother. She can make it up to Ed some day. She will only want the shop for a year or 2.

Kate thinks about Mrs. Moe's letter about a work-study job in TV. The letter said that Kate is good at working with her hands and with ideas. *That is not bad,* Kate thinks. If Mrs. Moe thinks she's that good at things, other people will think she is. Maybe Mrs. Moe will write another letter.

Then Kate thinks of May Louis. She will call her the second she gets back. Now she can be on "What's Happening" after all! Maybe everything will work out.

Kate starts to fall to sleep. But before she does that, she thinks about one more thing: Dan. Will he look her up when he moves to her town? She said she would not be there. But maybe he will try just the same. Maybe he will know that she went back. By then, she will be washed up and have a new shirt.

As Kate thinks, she looks at the groups of lights go by. They pass town after town. In 7 hours, she will see the night lights of her town.

Kate is happy to have things to look ahead to. Everything looks better than it did a week back. She laughs out loud. Some other people on the bus turn their heads to look at Kate. Who is this girl laughing out loud? They think she is out of it. Kate makes a face at them and then laughs some more. The people turn back to their books or sleep. Kate falls into a good, long sleep.

AFTER PAGE 10:

Write a word from the story in each space.

When Kate gets to _____ , all she has to do is find Willy.

The driver says, "You look like you are

_____ away!"

Kate thinks her big brother Ed is _____ .

Kate says, "I don't want _____ ."

Write the sentence that best says what the story is about so far.

Kate likes her room.

She hands back the $5.

Kate runs away to L.A.

_____

_____

AFTER PAGE 14:

Write these 4 sentences below. But write them in the order they happened.

Kate gets on a bus heading for L.A.

There has been a bad scene for 6 weeks.

Kate starts walking in L.A.

Someone is on her tracks.

_____

_____

_____

_____

_____

_____

_____

AFTER PAGE 20:

Circle the word groups below that describe Dan. Then write them in the spaces.

about 17 years old

so good-looking

27 years old

one of the "bad kids"

one of the "good kids"

_____

_____

_____

AFTER PAGE 24:

One of these sentences best says what the story is about. Write that sentence below.

L.A. is a big town.

Kate goes to find Willy.

Kate holds back her tears.

Maybe there is another.

_____

_____

AFTER PAGE 29:

Write these 4 sentences below. But write them in the order they happened in the story.

"I have a friend there," Kate says.

Kate looks in the phone book to find the Blue Root.

"Kate!" Willy calls out.

Kate walks into the Blue Root.

_____

_____

_____

_____

_____

_____

_____

AFTER PAGE 35:

Write a word from the story in each space.

So this is L.A. by _____ !

"Let's take Kate over to Chet's

_____ ."

Kate thinks that she will be more

_____ from now on.

AFTER PAGE 41:

Write these 4 sentences below. But write them in the order they happened.

Dot gives Kate a blanket.

Kate sees Sue Page on TV.

Dot says Kate can sleep at the Blue Root.

Kate falls off to sleep.

_____

_____

_____

_____

_____

_____

AFTER PAGE 45:

Write a word from the story in each space.

"You have photographs in _____ News?" Kate asks.

"We are by the street where _____ lives," Willy says.

No one in the _____ field would live in a house like that.

"You can't take _____ ," the woman screams.

AFTER PAGE 51:

Do you think that Willy will take Kate to see Sue Page? Why or why not? Circle your answer. Then find 3 sentences that back up what you think. Write them below.

I think Willy (will/will not) take Kate to Sue Page.

He does not know where Sue Page lives.
Willy has been so good to her.
Dot says, "That Willy!"
Sue Page is not a good friend of his.
Willy says, "It's been a long time."

_____

_____

_____

_____

_____

_____

_____

_____

_____

AFTER PAGE 57:

Write these 4 sentences below. But write them in the order they happened.

The kids look Kate up and down.

Kate sees her face in the window.

May Louis puts a $20 bill in Kate's hand.

Kate talks to May Louis.

_____

_____

_____

_____

_____

_____

_____

AFTER PAGE 63:

Write a word from the story in each space.

The man calls out at her _____ .

Kate says she has to get back to the

_____ _____ .

Kate looks for _____
in the Blue Root.

Now Willy talks_____
to Kate.

AFTER PAGE 70:

Write a word from the story in each space.

What if the man is a _____?

"I'm coming, _____," the man says and leaves.

"What a_____ !" Willy says to her.

Dot says, "I don't think you want to

_____ like these people at the Blue Root."

AFTER PAGE 77:

Circle the word groups below that describe how Kate looks now. Then write them in the spaces.

like a street woman   shirt is ripped

good-looking   not washed

like TV people   all washed

_____

_____

_____

AFTER PAGE 84:

Circle the word groups that describe how Kate feels at the end of the story. Then write them below.

feels like going to L.A.

feels like eating, sleeping, and washing

happy to see Willy

happy to have things to look ahead to

happy to see the Blue Root

_____

_____

_____

_____

(Go on to the next page.)

Write a word from the story in each space.

Kate feels like she can _____ for hours now.

Kate thinks about Mrs. Moe's letter about a work-study job in _____ .

Maybe Ed will let her have his

_____ like he said before.

One of these sentences best says what the end of the story is about. Write that sentence below.

There is a small wind.

Kate thinks maybe everything will work out now.

The people turn back.

Kate sees some people.

_____

_____

_____